Marcus Blakey Allmond

Fairfax, my Lord

A narrative poem

Marcus Blakey Allmond

Fairfax, my Lord
A narrative poem

ISBN/EAN: 9783743336827

Manufactured in Europe, USA, Canada, Australia, Japa

Cover: Foto ©Andreas Hilbeck / pixelio.de

Manufactured and distributed by brebook publishing software
(www.brebook.com)

Marcus Blakey Allmond

Fairfax, my Lord

CONTENTS.

THE CHASE.

UP the long length of "Gillet's Spur"
   The tired stag at noon-day went,
And full twain dozen dogs, at least,
   The forest echoes tore and rent.
He crossed the mountain's crown and sped
   On down the path that led below
To where the circling valley spread
   A wealth of summer's golden glow.
A thousand trees with life and leaf
   Were glad with hope and royal glee,
Along the trail the frightened stag
   Now chose his panting way to flee.

A thousand flowers bloomed and breathed
   Upon their beds of moss and loam;
A thousand birds with throats made glad
   The precincts of their forest home.
Still on and on the young stag ran
   Through winding woods, by forest streams,
While from the mountain top there rose
   The dogs' shrill yelps and huntsmen's screams.
Young Fairfax led the dashing crowd
   And Jules McMurdo followed near;
Sim Waldron next now bends him o'er
   And whispers in his horse's ear.
With whip and steel the riders rash
   Leap over rocks and rails and all,
And answer with a loud huzza
   The rushing hounds' far distant call,
Or wind a horn whose echoes shrill
   Adown the mountain's side now sped,
And reached the fleeing stag and filled
   His heart with yet a deeper dread.

The farm-house, white and large and strong,
  Embowered 'mid the shrubbery lay,
While oak and beech and hickory vied
  To keep the summer's sun away.
The mill-creek ran adown the vale
  And kissed the meadow-lands and sent
Its dewy breath along the hills
  Where corn-rows ran and swayed and bent;
And now far down the way it met
  "The Pond" and widened out and grew
To be a pretty lake whose waves
  Were, like the skies above them, blue.
The stag came onward at a pace
  That spoke his dread nor stopped nor stayed
Until he reached the farm-house where
  He sought the women, sore afraid.
Jean reached her lily arm and placed
  It 'round his neck in fond caress;
He eyed her with a look that said,
  "She'll rescue me in my distress."

(3)

Full many an hour had Jean and he
  Together roamed the woodlands o'er,
Full many a time upon the heights
  Stopped at some neighbor's open door;
Full many a time he'd circled 'round
  The pathway they had often gone;
But ne'er before had his good ear
  Caught dogs' deep cry or huntsman's horn.
"Be still my pretty deer," she said,
  "They shall not harm a single hair;
Your mistress loves you and will show
  These saucy huntsmen what you are."
The light shown in her deep brown eyes,
  Her chestnut locks were rich and neat,
Her cheeks were rosy, and her skin,
  A luscious hue, was soft and sweet.
She smiled and opened lips that were
  As cherries in the May-time seem.
Her pearly teeth were finer far
  Than poet ever yet could dream.

(4)

She laughed and rippling music fell
   In merry waves upon the ear.
She laughed, and when she did, she grew
   To all who heard her still more dear.
Cordelia by her side now stood—
   Anon she turned about and laid
Her hand upon the frightened deer—
   A pretty, blue-eyed city maid.
The dogs were coming down the side
   Of long *"No Business," and their cry
Drew near and nearer to the house
   With threats that meant to kill or die.
Cordele and Jean feared for their pet,
   And led it up the steps in rear,
Along the porch-way to the hall,
   Along the hall-way, and, in fear,
Up the long stair-way to the porch
   That crowned the front-view safe and high

* A Mountain in Virginia.

And looked o'er lowlands far and near
    And reaches of sweet azure sky.
The porch door closed, they stood and saw
    The hounds now rush across the vale,
And huntsmen dashing down the way
    Swift and yet swifter on the trail.
Cordele knelt down and put her arms
    About the deer's neck; Jean stood still
And watched the coming cavalcade,
    Prepared to meet them with stout will.
Her eyes flashed fire and lips were full
    Of ill-repressed emotion then;
She well could meet, and meeting, rout
    An even score or more of men.
The dogs came on and circled round
    The house and rested right below,
And sent their cries that rose and seemed
    As bent to bring the poor thing woe.
The huntsmen came at break-neck speed,
    And checked their horses, looked above

And saw the quarry they pursued
 Safe in the arms of tender love.
With lifted hats they craved them grace
 And got it right upon the spot;
The farmer bade them light and tie
 Their reeking horses piping hot.
Sim tipped a wink or two to Jules,
 But Fairfax cool ignored their sin,
And stately as a lord of old
 He led his retinue within.

ON THE LAKE.

*T*HE summer is a leal, good
         time
For those who have no anxious thought,
Who catch the sunshine in their hearts
    And hold it there when once 'tis caught,
Who meet and greet and smile and go
    And come again and bid adieu
With kindly feeling for the old
    And goodly welcome to the new,
Who ne'er grow old in life or heart,
    Come day or night, come weal or woe,
But take in good part all that comes
    And thank their stars that it is so.
Our huntsmen were a jolly set,
    And royally they took their glee—

To chase a stag upon the height
    Or woo a maiden on the lea.
The horses sought the meadows green,
    The masters sought the table long,
The dimpled maidens sat between,
    And all went merry as a song.
Cordele was soft and winning sweet,
    And Jean was stately in her grace,
And wit and humor, persiflage
    And sense found each its proper place.
The meal discussed, they then withdrew
    To where the spacious parlors were,
And music lent its subtle charm
    To while away the time with cheer.
"Cordele, Cordele," the cry went up,
    "Cordele, a song?" The blue-eyed maid
Then touched the keys and thus she sang
    The while her fingers nimbly played.

𝔖𝔬𝔫𝔤.

A stag came over the mountains, O!
A stag came over the mountains, O!
A stag came over the mountains, O!
    And the dogs came following after.
Three knights came over the mountains, O!
Three knights came over the mountains, O!
Three knights came over the mountains, O!
    I "carn't" sing now for laughter,
      Ha, ha, ha, ha, ha, ha, ha, ha,
    I "carn't" sing now for laughter.

When wolves are out and abroad, my dear,
When wolves are out and abroad, my dear,
When wolves are out and abroad, my dear,
    The lambs may look for danger.
I've something to tell, you had better hear,
I've something to tell, you had better hear,
I've something to tell, you had better hear,
    Beware, beware the stranger,
      Ha, ha, ha, ha, ha, ha, ha, ha,
    You had better beware the stranger.

Jules rose in well-feigned wrath and swore
  She wronged their knightly valor, and
He gave his arm and led away
  The little beauty from the stand.
They passed along the gravel walk
  On toward the lake's inviting brim,
And Jean and Fairfax followed suit—
  A maiden aunt attended Sim.
The sun was sinking in the west
  On downy beds of varied hues,
The length'ning shadows threw their arms
  Around the three embarking crews.
Cordele and Jules sped on ahead,
  Fairfax and Jean kept to the right,
Sim and the aunt—somewhat demure—
  Slow followed on, but still in sight.
Cordele was in her merry mood,
  And laughed and sang and talked and ran
Her hand along the water's top
  And dared whate'er a maiden can.

"I'm weary of the good and grand,
   I'm weary of the city's glare,
I would I were a bird and might
   Be free to skim the realms of air;
I'd like to do whate'er I choose,
   I'd like to go where e'er I please,
I'd like to say just what comes up
   And take the world in perfect ease.
A woman—aye! a woman, O!
   They've got me fastened up in stays,
They've got my feet encircled 'round
   With skirts that clog my path always.
O blasted bonds—a knife, a knife
   To cut them and to make me free.
My life, my all I offer—take—
   For one sweet breath of liberty.
I care not for the dread *'on dit'*
   That rules the world and makes it sin
To step beyond the beaten path
   And view the mysteries within.

Here's to thee, Mater Libertas,
  I raise thy standard and hurrah;
Peace to him who now sues for peace,
  For him who sues for war, here's war.
Cordele is free.   She bids adieu
  To all restraints of time or tide;
Come, speed the vessel straight ahead,
  And while we ride, why, let us ride."
Jules answered with a merry laugh
  And wicked twinkle in his eye:
"Fair sister of the Eastern land
  I welcome your philosophy.
Life is too short for serious things;
  The shadows lie along the ground,
The sunlight comes not every day,—
  Let's take it while it may be found.
'*Dum vivimus, vivámus,*' then,
  The motto of our mutual plight,
We twine the gilded light of day
  Around the gloomy form of night.

Speed, vessel, o'er the waters blue,
 Speed, vessel, and our song shall be
Henceforth, 'Hurrah for love and light,
 Hurrah for love and liberty.'"

* * * *

Fairfax and Jean were soberer folks;
 They talked of many noble things,
Of God and man and nature sweet,
 And all life's wondrous happenings.
He loved a jest, enjoyed a laugh,
 And chased a deer or winged a bird,
But still he loved the true and good,
 And most of all, God's Blessèd Word.
Whose heart is true can laugh as well
 As he whose heart is steeped in guile;
Whose lips are pure can be as glad
 As he whose words are reeking vile.
There is no clash between a song
 That gleams with merriment and glee

And that Sweet One who lived and died
  To bless the bleeding world and me.
The noble name that Fairfax wore
  Was passport to the country wide;
His presence at a farmer's door
  Made Jolly Welcome strut with pride.
This made the house he had drawn near
  So warm and cheery at his sight;
This gave to Jean the confidence
  To row abroad with coming night;
She felt that at the oar-locks sat
  A man whose soul was Honor's own,
Who ruled a realm far wider than
  A jeweled monarch on his throne—
Himself, a vast intelligence,
  Wide fields of thoughts and lands of dream,
The inner realms of consciousness;
  The hidden heavens which rounding gleam
With worlds on worlds within them set
  And beauties of unreckoned worth

That make a home of endless bliss
    Out of the humblest heart on earth.
Some natures are so nobly made
    We trust them with a perfect trust;
Some forms so grandly fashioned are
    We can't believe them made of dust.
They come at intervals as comes
    The bloom upon the century tree,—
Are Philip Sidney in one age
    And in another Robert Lee.
The seeds of their lives scattered through
    All the interstices of Time
Will flower and fruit in every age,
    On every shore, in deeds sublime.
Fairfax was one whom men revered,
    And women worshipped as a god;
A leader born, he seemed to own
    Each inch of ground on which he trod.
A subtle consciousness of worth
    Clothed all he did and all he said;

He feared no living man, and yet
  Oft bowed before a pretty maid.
He saw in woman's beauty glow
  The richest colors of the Hand
Whose skill artistic paints the world
  And makes the humblest floweret grand.
Her presence was a hidden song
  That thrilled him with a rich delight;
A breezy freshness clothed his form,
  His face put on a newer light.
When on his ear her accents fell,
  And on his sight there beamed her eye,
For her he'd bare his arm and fight;
  For her he'd win the day or die.
Hail heroes of the elder time!
  Hail knights that Arthur led of old!
Sir Galahad were worth to-day
  A thousand knights whose god is gold.
Fairfax now wound his horn, and lo!
  The three boats came from quarters wide,

And turned their prows the homeward way,
  Slow moving onward side by side.
Cordele, the blue-eyed, raised the song,
  And all joined in with merry glee;
The moon shone bright and sweet above,
  And touched them with her witchery.

THE DEPARTURE.

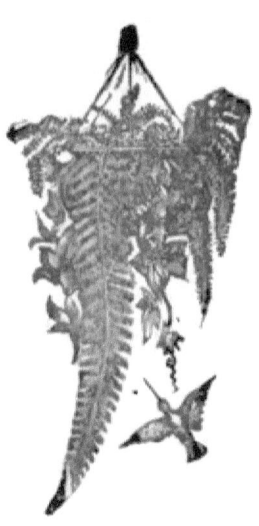

ᴛHE morrow on the hill-tops
  stood
    And sun-light shone upon her
      face,
The while her pretty smile would woo
  The huntsmen to another chase.
They gave their squires the word to bring
  Their champing steeds from stables near,
And, taking up their horns, they wound
  Their notes across the lowlands clear.
The answering cry of hounds arose
  As eager for the coming fray;
Cordele broke into song and held
  Her pretty cup in tempting way:

A Stirrup Cup.

"Are you ready for the chase, my lads,
  Across the circling plain?
Are you ready for the chase, my lads?
  Here's to you once again.
Lift the bugle, loose the leashes,
  Let your steeds now shake their mane,
But before you ply the spurs, my lads,
  Here's to you once again.

‚Are you ready for the chase, my lads,
  Upon the distant steep?
Are you ready for the chase, my lads?
  Here's to you long and deep.
May the maidens that await you
  Have no reason e'er to weep;
But before you ply the spurs, my lads,
  Here's to you long and deep.

Are you ready for the chase, my lads,
  Across the rivers wide?
Are you ready for the chase, my lads?
  Here's health, what e'er betide.
Lift the bugle, loose the leashes,
  And your noble steeds bestride;
But before you ply your spurs, my lads,
  Here's health, whate'er betide."

The huntsmen cheered with lifted hats
  And promised they would come again, —
Sank rowels in their gallant steeds
  And sped across the pretty plain.
The dogs were gone; their bayings deep
  Were heard upon the mountain's side
Up which our heroes clambered now
  With something of a martial pride.
The deeds of doughty prowess done
  Upon the eve of yesterday,
Within their hearts in fondest thought
  Are stored forever now away;
And, though they westward ride them now
  With manhood pulsing in each vein,
Jules dreams of Cordele's merry mood
  And Fairfax walks with Jean again.
They reached their homes and went their ways.
  The daily sun-rise came and went.
Days waxed to weeks, weeks waxed to months,
  And seasons with the seasons blent.

Who once have met may, if they wish,
   And naught prevent yet meet again,
Though mountains rise and surly threat
   The pretty poutings of the plain.

CREDE LYLE.

———

A SINEWY form, an eagle
eye,
A step elastic, and an arm
Of iron mould,—such was Crede
Lyle—
The owner of the neighboring farm.
An alien to these parts, he knew
The skill to make the harvest gleam
With glorious plenty and the grass
In velvet splendor clothe the stream.
As now he moved beneath the trees
And caught the wild flower from its stalk,
The boughs bent low and pricked their ears
To listen to his fitful talk:

"Her form is as a sculptor's dream,
  Her eye is magic's self and leads
Me as a captive and my heart
  For closer fellowship still pleads.
I know not what this force may be
  That lies within the inmost soul
And will not down, but reaches forth
  And holds the whole man in control.
I've simply met her as a friend
  Should meet a neighbor, yet I know
She's set my flood of feelings all
  Now toward her with impulsive flow.
A silent moon whose silver beam
  Falls o'er my being's rock-ribbed shore,
She lashes or allays its waves—
  Its mistress now and evermore."
An acorn from the tree now dropped;
  He turned his head; not far away
Upon a clump of moss-grown rocks
  A pretty deer was now at play,

Upon its neck great ribbons blue, —
　And ho! who's that who's just in sight—
A ray of sunlight hidden there
　Within this almost sylvan night?
He kept the path that brought him near
　And tipped his hat to lovely Jean,
Who smiled and wove the wild red-rose
　And cypress with the eglantine.
"I like this land," now Lyle began,
　"For nature here is lavish, and
Her bounties smiling group and bless
　The waiting eye on every hand.
I wandered many a good league forth
　To find a spot would charm my stay
Until I chanced on this, I love, —
　I hope—upon a lucky day.
The generous soil responds with glee
　To kindly treatment and my bins
O'erflow each year and life is passed
　Far from the great world's greater sins."

A cloud o'erspread his brow just then.
    His words provoked a sleeping thought;
To turn it off, he asked of Jean
    "What pretty thing was that she wrought?"
"Oh! just a nosegay," she replied,
    "Of wild flowers that I thought I'd make
For Tillie Dare, the invalid,
    Who lives down yonder by the lake.
And wont you help me just a bit?
    Be neighborly and get me now
That honey-suckle standing there,
    Those pretty leaves from off that bough."
Lyle answered now her every wish,
    And heaped the rock she sat upon
With all the gifts the forest has
    Until her kindly work was done.
Then on they moved and came at length
    To where the mill-creek turned the wheel,
And Tillie Dare lay pale and weak,
    Where sun-rays through the shadows steal

And try to cheer her lingering days
That need but little here below
Save human sympathy and love
To lighten with their tender glow.
Poor Tillie knew her days were few,
Yet repined not, but in good part
Bore her sad lot and gave to Jean
Warm thanks from out a grateful heart.
"How good you are to come and see
My flick'ring life hang quiv'ring here!
The smile you bring and kindly word
Fill me always with sunnier cheer.
Our lives are as the days that go,
Or bright with sun or dark with cloud.
They bring to men or weal or woe,
And bless or blight the circling crowd.
Blest is the life that's hid with God,
Whose pathway is a ray of light
To heal the stroke of Time's rough rod
And make the gloomy world's heart bright.

To him who living lifts his race
  To see and know the sweeter ways
Of his good Master, death is grace
  And plentitude of endless praise.
The wide circumference of soul
  That circles through the lives of men
To bless with fellowship the whole
  Finds death but life begun again.
God rules—the Maker of all things,
  He crowns the toiler with His rest—
A blessèd life in death still brings
  The blessing of all blessings best.
How envied then you, needs, should be
  By all whose lives your sweet life touch,
Not for the wealth that smiles around,
  But that your hand has done so much!
I soon must go, but from the skies
  I send my prayer that God may bless
The gentle heart whose gentle hand
  Relieves the stricken in distress."

Jean blushed and kissed the pallid brow;
   Lyle looked at Jean and thought, "I own
This is the queenliest woman that
   Was ever on or off a throne."
With kindly parting words they went
   Along the lake's o'ershadowed brim;
The pretty deer ran at their side,
   Or plunged into the lake to swim.
Lyle wished he had the will to say
   All his heart felt, but 't was in vain;
So he resolved he'd put it off,
   Until by chance they met again.
They talked as people who have read
   And travelled much are wont to talk,
And found when they had reached her home
   They each had had a pleasant walk.
The shades of eve were coming on,
   When Credo bade adieu and went
His homeward way with busy thoughts
   And head unconscious downward bent.

What thoughts he thought—what memories
   woke—
  I can not tell, I only know
His brow was pursed, his hand was clenched,
  He struggled with some hidden woe.
He muttered to himself strange words
  Of "fate" and "wrong" and "who could
   tell?"
When on his ear a cheery song,
  Yet tinged with sorrow, sudden fell.
He looked and there the cottage home
  Of Embry Duncan lay before,
And "Luce," his daughter, swung the churn
  And sang just out the vine-clad door:

The Swinging-Churn Song.

"Dapple Daisy down the meadow lowing coming back,
And the calf within the cowpen runs the beaten track.
Each is happy with the thinking of the meeting near,
But I sit and wait still wishing for thy coming, dear.

        Churn, go forward,
        Churn, go backward,
     While my song must be:
        Come, butter, come,
        Come, butter, come,
     And come, my love, to me.

Birds are singing gaily upon bush and tree;
Each as happy with its mate as a bird can be.
If they part a moment, they soon meet again;
But thy lingering, loved one, gives me endless pain.

        Churn, go forward,
        Churn, go backward,
     While my song must be:
        Come, butter, come,
        Come, butter, come,
     And come, my love, to me."

He shook his head as on he passed.

    "Sweet child," he thought, "you do not
        know

Nor ever will, I hope, the depths—

    The deepest depths of hidden woe.

The bloom is on your pretty cheek.

    Be patient and he'll soon be here.

The butter comes and so comes he

    To give you joy and share your cheer.

Who sighs for wider sweep of life

    But sighs for wider chance of wrong.

May all the 'endless pain' you have

    Flow forth, my pretty maid, in song,

And, while it sweetens your pent heart,

    Make glad the wings of neighboring air,

And bless alike the maker and

    The object of your gentle prayer.

For me, ah! well"—he crossed the creek,

    Passed through the gate and stood
        before

His home, reached out and turned the knob
Passed in and locked the heavy door.

TO ARMS.

STERN war arose. The rolling drum
  And shrill voiced fife were calling men
To arms! to arms! and tramping feet
  Throughout the land were heard again.
Fairfax rode o'er his acres wide,
  And viewed them in their laughing wealth.
His workmen met him with a smile,
  Rejoicing in their homes and health.
He sighed to think of what he'd read
  Of war and its destructive hand,

And wondered when the Master's love
Would bring sweet peace to every land.
He loved his country and her rights,—
His mother State far best of all,
And there resolved he'd draw no sword
Save at her most emphatic call.
But then, alas! too soon it came—
The tide of battle sweeping by;
He saw his State's dread jeopardy
And heard her to her children cry.
Along the vales, upon the hills,
Th' awakened farmers gathered then
And looked about them for a man—
The leader of his fellow-men.
All tongues cried out, "Fairfax, Fairfax"—
All eyes now sought him from afar.
Jules, Sim and hundreds more now came
To have him lead them forth to war.
He donned his uniform and sword
And mounted on his famous steed,

With will to meet the stoutest foe
   And heart to pity those who'd bleed.
Still more and more the throng increased
   Till all the old "militia ground"
Was filled with farmers, workmen, all
   Who lived for miles and miles around.
The drilling squadrons moved by day;
   The camp-fires glowed at fall of night;
The hearts of men seemed bent upon
   One thought alone "to fight, to fight."
Fairfax moved here and there and made
   Arrangements for th' unlettered crowd.
While in his sacred heart he bore
   A silent prayer, their talk was loud.
They clamored for the coming fight
   And revelled in the thought of gore;
He prayed within his heart for peace—
   For peace and brotherhood once more.
For war is war, terrific and
   The hand of passion running mad,

The woe of woman and the worst
　　Of foes a child has ever had.
The savings of unnumbered years,
　　The guidings of a father's hand,
The generous promptings of the heart
　　When peace and plenty fill the land;
These in wild flames are swept away,
　　And on the coming youth is thrown
The harvest of unnumbered woes,
　　Thick through the coming morrows sown.
This Fairfax knew and on his brow
　　Care stamped her wrinkle, and his heart
Was heavy with the woes he knew
　　Were War's own bitter, bounden part.
Alone upon his matchless steed
　　Across the hill, across the plain,
And o'er the mountains was he come
　　To sweet "Glen-Mary" once again.
Jean met him with a smile of peace,
　　A hand that good, warm welcome gave;

But sorrowed at his serious brow
   And martial manner stern and grave.
At hour fitting forth they went,
   Beneath the overhanging trees,
In quiet chat of events which
   Would soon be winged across the seas.

CORDELE.

HE smoke was hanging thick
and grim
Above the city's throbbing
heart,
Where pulsed the blood of traffic and
Where pined in poverty High Art.
The greedy herd moved on and bowed
With one accord to Mammon's sway,—
With vice they thrilled the heart of night,
With painted virtue cheated day.
A pretty mansion rising high
Upon a noted thoroughfare—
A cosy chamber—windows wide—
And Cordele reading sitting there;—

This is the picture, and we hear
   The words she reads—this blue-eyed
      belle—
"I come, Cordele, the war is on;
   I come, my love, to bid farewell."
"He comes—dear Jules! He comes, and I
   Shall scatter roses in his way.
My father's wealth shall gild the night
   And frame in joy the fleeting day.
He's made it and I know not how.
   He gives it time he ne'er gave me.
I'll spend it as I get a chance
   In many a jolly jamboree.
Come, Jules, soul of my soul, and we,
   My naughty soldier-boy, shall sound
The depth of every jollity,
   That in this city may be found.
So that I drink the bumper full
   The present moment gives, I care

No whit for all the after moons
    That wax and wane, however fair.
The heart that built this mansion grand
    Knows nothing of those softer things
(The goody good will prate of them)
    About which every poet sings.
He laughs to scorn these Christian thoughts,
    And I but echo in my heart
The thoughts that days and months and
      years
    Have been of him the larger part.
Here's to thee, sweet Utility,
    His end and aim the dollar is,
Mine is my pleasure and I find
    That mine is mine, since his is his.
Servant, ahoy! bring up the cup
    Thy master drinks his wine from, I
Will see if I can quench my thirst
    As he does often when he's dry.

Bring me a 'Ouida.'   Let me read
   Of gilded sin as virtue rare.
If callers ring, tell them, I pray,
   I've gone a driving—anywhere.
So that I get my ease, I care
   But little for this social whir
That money buys.   Sweet Voluptas,
   I am your loving worshipper.
Come, Jules, and join me and we'll find
   Two hearts that beat for aye as one;
Here's to thee, con amore, mine—
   A bumper, once, twice, thrice, I've done."

REVENGE.

CREDE LYLE was reared upon
the lap
Of Luxury, and his life had
lain
Amid a stormy war of words
  Wrought by the miser-heart of Gain.
Nor had the conflict stopped with words,
  But Passion stirred the pistol's flame;—
A human life was offered up
  To satisfy fell Anger's claim.
His mother was a vengeful soul
  Who ne'er forgave a conceived harm,
But nursed her wrath against the day
  She could assuage it with her arm.

Hamilcar-like she led her charge—
  A dimpled boy—and made him swear
Eternal vengeance on each head
  Her caprice chose just anywhere.
Enough she had to squander far
  In idle chance and yet her greed
Still clamored more and more for more
  Than any human soul could need.
An honored name was linked in trade
  With her dead husband's, and she
      dreamed
A wrong was wrought her, and her eye
  At mention of that good name gleamed.
The wordy war had lingered on
  In suit with suit in common law,
Till Justice cast it out at length,
  And stirred her with its solemn awe.
She took redress unto herself
  And, leading by his hand her boy,

She made him fire the fatal shot
    That slew a household's tender joy—
The gentlest of his race and best—
    The eldest of the Fairfax name,
Whose fancied wrong she'd laid away
    And nurtured as a holy flame.
The hand of Law had siezed and placed
    Her frenzied soul in "durance vile;"
For life, the nation's guardians thought
    It best to house her witless guile.
For safety's sake Crede went elsewhere;
    But she had nursed his wrath to flame
And urged and urged him ne'er to leave,
    On her cursed soul, one of that name.
One day he heard Jean mention—what?
    The Fairfax name and speak its praise.
His heart leaped high and passion stirred
    As it had stirred in other days.
She told him of the coming war—
    The tramp of men and loud alarms—

The flocking of the freemen all
  In answer to the call to arms.
And, when he learned that Fairfax led
  The embattled hosts, his spirit stirred
To lead his foes and meet him yet,—
  But still he spoke no bitter word.
Henceforth in vale and mountain dell
  He sought for comrades for his flag,
And trained them to the use of arms
  On lowland leas and upland crag.
For one fell purpose they were called—
  A holy one to him he dreamed;—
To slay a wrecker of his home,
  Each drawn and sharpened sword now
    gleamed.
He tutored them in sweet revenge,
  And told them of his mother's wrongs.
They mixed their anger in their cups
  And sang it in their battle songs.

IN PERIL'S GRASP.

WHEN Fairfax now at
    that calm hour
  Forth 'neath the trees
    walked arm in arm
With pretty Jean, he never dreamt
  An eye was near that meant him harm.
Crede Lyle, as fate would have it, walked
  In meditative mood along,
And every thought was teeming now
  With something of his fancied wrong,
When suddenly he saw quite near
  Two forms majestic moving on;
He stepped from off the path and stood
  Behind the heavy scented thorn.

Too deep their thoughts imbedded were
 In events fraught with thousands' fate
To scan the pretty landscape for
 The nurser of a hidden hate.
Lyle's eye was gleaming and his heart
 Was beating as 't would burst in twain.
His passion ebbed and flowed and ebbed
 And flowed and ebbed and flowed again.
He took his pistol—cocked it—raised
 His hand and took deliberate aim;
Jean moving on and talking soft
 Unconscious now between them came.
"Poor human beings," thus she spoke,
 "There is, I think, enough of woe
In this sweet world for men who're men
 To stop and think and know it's so,
Before they draw their swords and try
 To hew each other and make moan
For thousands who on either side
 Are doubly dear unto their own.

There was a time when Odin ruled
  And Högni's heart on dish was laid
And served to Gunnar and he smiled
  With calm sweet joy as sooth he said:
'The heart of Högni by the side
  Of timid Hialli's heart has rest;
It trembles little in the dish,
  It trembled less while in his breast.
I'll roast and eat it—drink its blood
  To give my heart a stouter stroke,
And teach my hand a readier skill
  To wield the knife or club of oak.
My happiness in battle lies.
  Red slaughter is the soldier's part.
Ah! what is sweeter than the blood
  Drunk warm from out a foeman's heart?'
But Christ is come. Peace and good-will,
  These are the new world's corner stones.
For every woe a glad, new joy
  And healing hands for broken bones.

Fie on the man who can not bear
  A wrong and right it with a good!
Shall all the centuries come and go
  And lift us to no better mood?
Does Odin reign that any now
  Should batten on a brother's woe?
Christ finds a kinsman hidden there
  Beneath the jacket of a foe.
Come, men, be *men* and right your wrongs
  As *men* with *men* should right them now,
With Christ's love warm within your hearts
  And Christ's truth written on your brow."
Crede Lyle heard all her sweet voice spoke;
  He dropped his pistol by his side.
They walked on quite unconscious still
  Amid the forests sweeping wide.
What Fairfax said in his response
  Was what a man of honor should.
Crede turned upon his heel and went
  Straight on and out the brooding wood.

"For her dear sake I let him live,
   I yet shall wing him on the way.
He knows not that a tiger lies
   Close by to spring upon its prey."
At once he sped him to the home
   Of Embry Duncan and conferred
Upon the time of rendez-vous—
   The speeding of the clarion word
That was to gather from the dells,
   The crags high up the mountains' side,
The swift hands that could wing a hawk
   Or split the panther's fluffy hide.
And as he talked with Embry there
   Luce sat a spinning in the room,
Or gathered from the pretty grass
   The leaves, new fallen, with her broom.
She listened to their plans and felt
   Her blood creep cold in every vein.
They spoke of death. Her father's name,
   Her lover's now she heard again.

What, if her father fell in fight?
　　What, if her lover died too soon?
These bitter thoughts ran through her mind
　　And chilled her all the afternoon.

THE GALA–NIGHT.

'TIS presto and we make a
    change
  To where the city's surging
    tide
Flows streaming through its
    thoroughfares
'Neath lights that flare and flicker wide.
Here stands apart sad squalor now—
  A home where horror loves to dwell,
That reeks with all the vices and
  The passions of an earthly hell.
Now yonder is a pale, sweet child
  That drinks the germs of death that lie
Upon the stench of stagnant pools
  That turn the nose and fret the eye.

Beyond, the car-bells jingle clear
    Upon the air.   Anon the gleam
Of rich electric arcs that pour
    Their pretty lights in constant stream.
The bawd's loud laugh re-echoes now
    Her victim's bitter charge and see
The erring lad now staggers by—
    A dupe to wine's sad witchery.
An open door; the blind awry;
    A wretch within with lifted cup;
An oath; a burly form that sits
    Swift from its seat now rises up;
A dagger gleams; we pass along.
    Two porters bear a burden here;
A beggar lifts her hand and pleads
    With quivering voice and falling tear;
Three wagons go in hurried rush;
    A lad belated cries the news;
A shopman takes and stores away
    A string of antiquated shoes;

Two merchants arm in arm now walk
   Upon this better thoroughfare;
A maiden and a youth make love
   Just at the foot of this broad stair;
A couple—richly clad and prim—
   Pass on to see the famous play;
A carriage with its owner comes—
   A pretty chestnut and a gray;
A loiterer lingers 'long the street
   Pries in the windows, scans them long;
An urchin, ragged, happy faced,
   Breaks into snatches of sweet song.
The noise grows less and less and now
   The yards lie round the mansions, and
The eye beholds a sweeping stretch
   Of massive structures rising grand.
The trees in leaf, the flowers in bloom,
   The grasses soft and rich and green,
And fountains playing pretty streams
   At intervals now set between,

Make all the air as fresh and sweet
   As grottoes of the pretty fay
Who revels in fair Nature's lap
   Upon a charming summer day.
Here rising up was Cordele's home—
   A flood of light, a breathing bower
Of wondrous beauty, wreathed and sweet
   With bunting and with blooming flower.
A gala-night she makes it now,
   And crowds of friends are streaming in.
Erelong the waiting ear is glad,—
   The baton bids the ball begin.
The pretty dancers come and go
   Like fire-flies on the meadow-land
Or swells of dashing billows that
   Roll up and off the sea-swept sand.
The gleam of gold, the brilliant flash
   Of diamond and encircling pearl
Adorn alike the matron and
   The pretty stripling of a girl.

The silk and satin gleam and mix
   With tulle and brocade and fine lace,
Each pretty color 'ranged to make
   More pretty still each pretty face.
And arms and necks and shoulders rise
   In rounded plumpness quite as fair
As snow-flakes on their gentle way
   From out the realms of upper air.
"O Life! O Life!" sighed Cordele as
   She rested now within the arm
Of Jules, whose gaze she riveted
   As with a subtle, ceaseless charm.
He never saw her eye so blue,
   The color on her cheek so rare,
Such pretty, golden, shimmering light
   Enmeshed within her glorious hair;
Nor heard her laugh as waters pour
   Such rippling music on his ear;
Nor felt her pretty little foot
   Trip 'round him half so light and clear.

The modiste and the maid had both
    Conspired with Nature for a form,
Would sweep his very breath away
    And take his whole heart as by storm.
If e'er before there was a doubt
    Of his surrender to her wiles,
It now forever dissipates
    Beneath the magic of her smiles.
And she—ah! she, this paragon,
    This thing of beauty made to please,
Yon looker-on can never dream
    That such as she are ill at ease;
But where the music's pretty call
    Floats to the ear and all things seem
As happy as a heart can be
    Are troubles we may never dream.
Cordele has had her stubborn way,—
    The dancers come, the dancers go;
Their nimble feet are dancing time
    Unto her everlasting woe.

The heart-aches and the pangs that be
    Amid the revels of the dance,
Thank God! are hidden from the view
    Of all save His all-seeing glance.
And those who see sweet beauty's spell
    And gladden at its witchery,
May never know the things that are
    Or. dream the things that are to be.
God rules and He alone should know
    The Future and the Future's will;
For He alone can put His arms
    Around us and can save us still.

NOUS VERRONS.

ANOTHER day was
come and now
Fairfax prepared to
bid adieu.
His horse stood at the
great front gate;
He lingered as most lovers do.
Upon the heights Lyle ranged his troop
And from an out-post, glass in hand,
Bent forward scanning with his eye
The reaches of out-lying land—
He sees the horse, the rider sees,
And turning bids his comrades know
Their prey is moving o'er the plain
Which they had left an hour ago.

"No fooling when the moment comes.
   Strike death to him and that right sure.
He'll cross my path and thwart my plans
   With his dread presence never more."
Unconscious of the lurking fate
   His hidden foe held for him now,
Fairfax rode o'er the rich, brown road
   That clambered to the hillock's brow
Then darted down and lay between
   Great stretches of sweet clover-field,
And rose again where waving oats
   Unto wide sweeps of orchard yield.
The blue-bird caroled on the limb;
   A lazy vulture sailed o'er head;
A rabbit stealing from the field
   Now up the roadway startled sped;
A cottage home soon comes in view;
   A bevy of gray geese now hiss;
A barking dog jumps at the fence,
   And at the window sits a miss;

The creek beyond runs o'er the stones
   And deepens at the neighboring ford;
Two oxen quench their raging thirst,
   Worn hot beneath the heavy load;
The driver bows and keeps his eye
   Upon the stately horseman's form,
Takes off his hat and with his cloth
   Wipes his tanned brow now reeking
      warm;
The sunlight lay on grasses sweet
   With subtle perfumes, and the air
Was rich with exhalations that
   Rose up to greet him everywhere.
His mind was busy with the calls
   Stern Duty placed upon his brow;
His heart for peace was longing, but
   His country's thoughts were other now.
Himself he needs must relegate
   Unto the rear, and bare his blade

To breast the issue that was come
    And he himself had never made.
Still on he rode and pistols clicked
    Upon the height impatient still,
And daggers gleamed and glowed to think
    They soon would have their own sweet
        will.
Thus down the road of life we move
    And know not what before us lies
Until, ere we have dared to dream,
    We face some sudden, sad surprise.
For us whose eye is on the height
    And heart is with the rider true,
There lurk in ambuscade e'en now
    Old Death and all his mystic crew.
We drink the floods of neighb'ring air,
    And catch the bird's song in our ear;
We spur our jade and whistle out
    And ever come more near and near;

We laugh, as laugh we should, and feel
  As one who owns an endless day;
We take our golden hours and spill
  Their glad sweet wealth along the way.
The monster lurks and whets his blade
  And licks his tongue in horrid glee.
Ah! well, if serious thought were mixed
  With all our merry minstrelsy.
For lo! where turns the roadway here
  A hand lies on the bridle now,
And Fairfax—stop, stay, is it Death
  That mantles o'er his noble brow?
Was that a flight of whistling balls?
  Is that the gleam of daggers high?
A struggle as of one who knows:
  "I win, I live; I lose, I die?"
No. Gentle Lucy lifts her eyes
  And pleads the stranger keep the right,
The foot-path that will bring him safe
  Around the dizzy, beetling height.

"Good friend, my father is up there
  And Mr. Lyle and he I love.
They wait to slay you, so they say,
  Wait up the road there, just above.
And oh! who knows but when they all,
  The many others, leap and strike,
My father's or my lover's form
  May lie upon the rocky pike?
In here and quickly 'round them ride,
  For my sake, please, sir, wont you now?
That's right.   God bless you.   You are
    kind;
  Some day I'll pay you, friend, some
    how."
Fairfax had read within her face
  The truth, as in the light of day,
"Guerillas whom her childish fear
  Has robbed," he thought, "now of their
    prey."

And in he rode as one who knows
  The bravest are least quick to dare,
Unless stern Duty, glory-crowned,
  Stands pointing while she whispers
    "There."
And Luce dashed from the roadway down
  And quick stole still through bending
    trees,
And coming to her little room,
  Fell there upon her maiden knees,
And prayed her God to save that one
  Whose heart was plighted to her own,
And bring him back to dwell with her,
  And be for her and her alone.
Oh! tender, pretty maiden thoughts!
  Oh! first love, how the after years
Will mock you with their hollow laugh;
  In secret bless you 'mid their tears;
Stretch out their arms and cry in pain.
  "Oh! for the blessèd days I knew,

Oh! for the sun-light that then clad
The whole world in its golden hue."

IN HIS VINEYARD.

"GLEN MARY."

ALONG the vale Jean passed
    and bore
    Her blessings to unnumbered
      poor,
    Or scaled the ruggéd heights
      and stood
A welcome guest before the door.
The landscape laughing in its glee,
    The song of bird on soaring wing,
The leaflets on the bending tree,
    The waters gurgling from the spring,
The varied hues of morn and eve,
    That clothed the east or western sky,

The rainbow resting on the peaks,
　The sunlit shower passing by,
The grasses ranging o'er the fields
　And vieing with the oats and wheat,
The hedge-rows hugging close the road,
　The sylvan wild-flowers at her feet,
The loving faith her young deer showed
　When in her lap its soft head lay;—
All these were chapters in a book
　That made her better every day.
Through Nature up to Nature's God
　Her soul now leaped with subtle song;
The Hand that made us is all right,
　It's we, good friends, who are all wrong.
And from the cross the message comes:
　"I am the way, I am the light:
Peace and good-will upon the earth,
　And day will dawn upon the night,
And woe that lurks from sun to sun
　And nestles in the human breast,

Will yield to peace—sweet peace that gives
  To His belovéd endless rest.
Not as the world knows is that peace
  That broods in gentle calm above
The heart that God has touched and filled
  With his serener, better love.
No gnawing tooth of bitter greed,
  No memory of a plotted wrong,
Cuts endless in its inner core
  Or stills the voice of happy song;
But, if the world's low treasures fly,
  The days serenely move them still,
For all things work for good to those
  Who know and do God's loving will,
And seek to scatter little bits
  Of secret goodness 'long their way
And lead the waning night of Greed
  Into Love's broader, sweeter day.
For newer, fuller light upon
  The problems of our daily need,

This is the statesman's higher work,
　This is the churchman's better creed.
Not gleaming treasures garnered up
　By wrecking of a human soul
Is wealth, but wealth is making good
　And glad the circle you control.
The rock that lies to splinter wide
　Your neighbor's child's fair tiny ship,
With higher strength remove and give
　The little tar a safer trip;
And, when the tropic seas are his,
　Let him in fair return make sure
He lade his ship in part for you,
　And bless you with his precious store.
Thus age for youth makes life more sweet,
　And youth holds up the agéd hand,
And each shall turn his happy feet
　Unto the sweeter, better land."
So Jean now thought and every where
　Her smiling face and gentle love

And tender hand and timely gift
  Her needing fellows bent above.
She gave to one a kindly word,
  Another labor for the day,
Another meat, and then she'd bend
  Here with another—bend and pray.
A pretty book the young child got;
  A new frock for the growing maid;
A weary mother had a "help;"
  The farm-hand's doctor's bill was paid.
But ever yonder was a thought
  With one on the embattled plain.
She prayed her God that He might send
  Peace to her countrymen again.

TO EACH HIS WAY.

BEYOND the mountains far
    away
  The captains of unnumbered
    hosts
  Were busy at their routine
    work;
  The soldiers—each—were at
    their posts.
In every heart there lay the thought
  For country it is sweet to die,—
This cheered the lonely sentry's step
  And brightened every leader's eye.
One heart was touched with purpose grand;
  One mind was bent to weave a plan

Would win the day and gain them peace,
 Nor cost them yet another man.
That soul was Fairfax and he knew
 Each by-path of the country 'round.
He ran his thoughts in circuit out
 And chose for him his battle-ground.
Slow days moved on by slower nights;
 His foemen grew impatient now.
They fancied cowards in their front,
 And offered to the gods a vow
To lash them with the willow's twigs
 And pull their noses in their face,
Since they had dipped their manhood in
 The cess-pools of a black disgrace;
But Fairfax let them fret and fume,
 With brow serene and heart that knew
The Future yet would parcel out
 The blatant soldier from the true.
The night came down the mountain heights
 And rested on the restless foe,

Whose careless eye had ceased to guard
　As once it guarded long ago.
When morning dawns, a flag slow moves
　Along the vale; the couriers stay
Just where the lazy general still
　Now wrapped in slumber snugly lay;
"Your further fight is useless now,"
　Thus spoke the spokesman in his ear,
"Your past is glorious, but your doom
　Is sealed.　I beg you listen, sir."
He showed him then the workings of
　The master-mind that planned the whole,
And further that the power once his
　Had now passed on from his control.
To lengthen now the fight was just
　A waste of human lives, and so
'T were best to yield his sword and own
　The war was done, and turn and go
Once more to happy homes where wives
　And children with their loving arms

Would welcome now their safe return
  From cruel war and war's alarms.
So ran the compact and, forsooth,
  The gladdened victors tried to see
How they could heal the wounded pride
  Wrought by their royal victory.
The vanquished smiled and proffered hands,
  All save one sullen chieftain who
With his sworn comrades picked his chance
  And from the mingling hosts withdrew.
As some fierce bird of prey which slips
  The snare that held a moment fast,
From crag to crag his flight he takes
  As crag with crag is swiftly passed,
And yonder where his aerie is
  He rests a moment from his flight,
Then swoops to fright the heart of day
  And batten on his spoil at night;
So Lyle now climbed the slumb'rous heights
  And sought secure a hiding place,

Still vowing vengeance in his heart
And wearing battle in his face.

SIMPLICITY.

A SOFT wind played adown the vale
    And toyed with the clover bloom,
Peered in amid the tangled grass,
    And whispered o'er the tawny broom,
Caught in its arms the humming bee,
    And put to flight the butterfly,
And kissed the tulip's pretty lips
    And jonquils as it passed them by.
It wreathed its young hands in the scent
    Of honeysuckles hanging near,

And touched the touch-me-not and said:
   "Now, jump, you pretty little dear."
It clambered up the hugh grape-vine,
   And shook the big leaves in great glee,
And whispered to a lady-bug,
   "Are you here? I have got you. See."
Then glanced below and caught a sight
   Of Luce close by the cottage now,
And jumped and put a pretty kiss
   Right on her pretty little brow.
Then oped its eyes. Lo and behold!
   Luce stroked her kitten on her knee,
And this was what the breeze then heard
   And wondered what it all could be.

Lucy's Complaint.

"If you loved a little Kitzie
  And he was afar away,
Would you be so happy, Kitzie,
  Happy as you are to-day?
        Kitzie-cat,
        Tell me that.

If you loved a little Kitzie,
  And a cruel huntsman came
With his gun to shoot him, Kitzie,
  Would you love him just the same?
        Kitzie-cat,
        Tell me that.

If you loved a little Kitzie,
  Would you weep and wish him here,
Would you write a letter, Kitzie,
  Would you call him home, my dear?
        Kitzie-cat,
        Tell me that."

Then a tear broke from her eye-lid
   And ran coursing down her cheek,
And her little lips now quivered
   And they could no longer speak.
Then the thoughtless little breeze
   That had laughed through all the day,
Bent and with a tender prayer
   Kissed the little tear away—
Put its arms about her form,—
   Laid her on its smitten breast,
Lulled her wearied little heart
   With its sweetness into rest,
Slowly stirred her from her thoughts,
   Taught her labor gives relief
When the pent and weary heart
   Bends beneath its heavy grief.
And she rose and went her way
   Where the field-road ran along;
As she passed the apple-tree
   Hummed herself a little song:

"Love and trust
        And God will bless you.
Wait, my heart.   It's bound to be.
        God is good
        And wont distress you,
If you'll wait, my heart, and see;
If you'll wait, my heart, and see.

.

Once my little Kitzie lingered
    And I thought '"T will surely die,'
And I prayed my God to save her
    And he saved her by and by.

    Love and trust
        And God will bless you.
Wait, my heart.   It's bound to be.
        God is good
        And wont distress you,
If you'll wait, my heart, and see;
If you'll wait, my heart, and see."

SOLDIER, ON!

THE fame of Fairfax filled the land.
　　He stole him for a moment's rest
To fair "Glen Mary," where he owned
　　The sweet surroundings suited best.
When woes have gathered thick and fast
And dark skies bend our path above,

What place so sweet? What heart so true,
As is the home, the heart we love?
When Victory wreaths with bays our brows
And Fame bedecks our path with flowers,
Our first thought is the home and heart—
The home and heart we know is ours.
And thither with a loving tryst
   We make our way unto our own
Far from the thoughtless crowd, whose
     shout
   Attends the victor's path alone,
As ready as the surly hound
   To fall upon a fallen prey
That its long tongue with bitter gibes
   Has tried to fell the live-long day.
One thought now pursed his master brow—
   The serried band upon the height,
Yet bent to break his country's laws
   And eager for the bloody fight.

He sought to know the chieftain's heart
  And learn the motive of his hate,
And bring him to his country's fold
  Repentant, if repentant late.
Jean fathomed all for him and told
  The story of Crede Lyle's sad life,
Just as she heard it told by one
  Who was an arch insurgent's wife.
Fairfax passed from his day's repose
  And took the reins in hand again,
With firm resolve to meet his foe
  And close at once his last campaign.
Around him lay the camp fires now
  On hill and dale, a pretty sight,
And in his tent he sat with brow
  O'er shadowed by the coming night.
To win and wound not was the thought
  That to his heart was still most dear,
When through the gloaming stole a song
  And fell upon his listening ear.

Soldier, On!

Darkness comes without our wishing.
　We must bear as best we may,
Knowing that its stars will light us
　To a brighter, better day.

Cheer thy heart and bid it "Courage!"
　Through the gloaming to the dawn.
Holy angels bend and beckon,
　While they whisper, "Soldier, On!"

Hero of our daily being,
　Bearing wounds for Honor's sake,
Let thy heart be glad within thee,
　Soon the roseate dawn will break ;—

Soon the songs of birds will echo
　In the valleys far and near,
And the world all robed in splendor
　Out of darkness will appear.

He who bears the lonely watchings
　Of the night of gloom alone,
Is the first who sees the day-king
　Seated on his golden throne.

Cheer thy heart and bid it, "Courage!"
  Through the gloaming to the dawn.
Holy angels bend and beckon,
  While they whisper, "Soldier, On!"

CORDELE.

THE busy wheels of Traffic roar
 And clatter on the list'ning ear;
The columns of black smoke ascend
 Yet up and up and disappear.
The teeming crowds are jogging, each
 In wild pursuit of hoarded pelf;
And all seem bent alone upon
 "The bread and cheese upon the shelf."
One lifts his mansion costly grand
 With millions in his coffers by,

Yet rushes as impelled by fate
  To make yet more before he die;
Another sees and knows the thirst
  For wealth can never get its fill,
But follows swift upon its track
  And swifter and yet swifter still.
As in some whirlpool swimmers strive
  To stem the billows and to rise
Each o'er his fellow to a height
  Will face the frontlet of the skies,
And fear to leave the stroke unmade
  Lest haply they may sink to doom
And flounder as a soggy log
  Ignobly to a watery tomb;
So here within this bustling mart,
  Each on this thronged and narrow street
Now toils, yet finds no stay nor rest,
  No place for tired brain and feet.
Each day he speeds as though the life
  Of millions hung upon his speed;

He gets and gets and gets and gets
  And finds he is still more in need.
When night comes on and morning stars
  Rise sweet within the eastern skies,
He goes to bed but downy sleep
  Is still a stranger to his eyes.
In visions of his fevered thought
  The game runs on, "I win, I lose."
He is the victim of the fate
  The thoughtless thousands rashly
    choose;
For in his house this day and hour
  The child whose all, his all's to be,
Sobs with a heart that moans to know
  Wealth is not loving sympathy.
For through the past years sown full
    thick
  Are hours she needed his heart's beat
To soothe and soften and his hand
  To lead her wicked little feet.

If haply wilful she essayed
    His will to thwart, he shook his fist
And swore an oath.   She passed from
        sight
    And went where her rash heart might
        list,
And did whate'er her angered pride
    And spiteful turn might deem her will.
Her busy father thought to soothe,
    If he would only foot each bill.
And so she ran the round of all
    An aimless life of pleasure hath,
And doubling on her track she came
    All weary down the olden path.
And sighed for rest and sighed for peace
    And raised to God her feeble prayer,
That some good hand would lead her
        heart
    From out these realms of dark
        despair—

These shades where strove in useless strife
 The poverty-stricken rich who need
For ill-fed minds and hungry souls
 The hale food of the Christian creed.
She fell on sleep and dreams there came
 Of rescue and of peace at last,—
Of tender words and gentle arms
 Around her shrinking figure cast.
She woke to find her throbbing brow
 On Jean's good heart.   She raised her
  eyes;
"Where did you come from? Surely,
  God
 In love has sent you from the skies.
Oh! Jean, this wayward world does wrong
 To think its heart can e'er find rest
Save in His arms, save in His love,
 Save on His sympathetic breast.
I've run the round. I know it all.
 It's hollow mockery they call fun.

There is no joy like that they know
 Who say, 'O God, thy will be done.'
Good friend, I love to hear your heart
 Sing its sweet music in my ear.
Methinks my weary soul would like
 To breathe its worthless self out here.
You know 'way down the by-gone days,
 I half-way dreamed of love and truth
And all those pretty things you've known,
 And decked your life with from your
  youth.
But oh! the chilling air of greed,
 Th' insatiate maelstrom, more and more
Swept my frail bark upon the seas
 Far from that balmy blessèd shore.
And I have lived—God pity me—
 God pity me and send me rest.
Jean, hold me closer, wont you, dear?
 Still closer to your loving breast.

Oh! could I die just here and now,
  I think I surely would be blest.
Jean, hold me closer, wont you, dear?
  Still closer to your loving breast.
Oh! This is good. The storm-tossed bird
  Is once again within its nest.
Jean, hold me closer, wont you, dear?
  Still closer to your loving breast."

THE COMBAT.

WHERE beetling crags on crags arise,
A bitter heart now longs for fight.
His 'leaguered hosts with restless step
Speed loit'ring day, curse coming night.
With heartless taunt they cry to know
Why those whose bulwarks rise on high
Meet not on mid-way ground and fight
Like men and win the day or die.
The patient Fairfax heard it all
And ran the problem through his mind,

"This is a private grievance and
    A private settlement should find.
Why need the hundreds who are here
    Spill their life-blood—a useless fate?
He does my country public wrong,
    Because he bears me private hate.
I'll meet him and let God and skill
    Decide at once what they deem best."
Then peaceful as a pretty babe,
    The guileless chieftain seeks his rest.
When morning came, a flag ascends
    The topmost peak—a parley pleads—
Crede Lyle consents on testy ground
    That Fairfax quickly state his needs.
Mid-way the hosts, the stainless knight
    Asks that his foe give reason why
As man with man they can not bring
    Their quarrel to an end.   The eye
Of Lyle flashed fire and his teeth
    Shone as a tiger's keen and white.

"There is but one thing, sir, to do—
   And that thing is to draw and fight."
"Agreed," said Fairfax, "if you'll make
   This compact: All on either side
Must swear they will abstain from fight
   And by the issue then abide.
And, if I fall or if I win,
   One thing alone of yours and you:
To yonder flag henceforth and now
   You swear forever to be true."
This then they swore and heralds made
   The wide announcement to the ranks.
On either side the cheers went up
   Like waters roaring over banks.
The seconds then prepared the swords
   And tested them of steel approved.
Then to and fro like ushers now
   Upon a gala-day they moved.
Had then a traveller happened by
   And seen affairs just as they stood—

He'd thought two friendly parties here,
 On hunt intent, met in the wood,
Nor known that sword with sword would
  . cross,
 And on it all depend the woe
Or weal of those who'd met in fight
 One for his land, one 'gainst his foe.
But so it was; Fairfax's heart
 Was lifted to his God in prayer
For all the hosts that circled round
 And all their loved ones every where;
Nor did he fail to ask that He
 Would shield his Jean from every harm,
And, knowing then his Duty called,
 He found him with a steady arm.
For prayer puts courage in the heart
 And steadies every patriot's hand
To strike for home and all that's dear—
 The God we love and native land.

Then quiet as a friend would go
  To meet a friend, peace on his face,
He moves to meet the Lyle half-way
  And shake his hand with knightly grace.
Swords then were crossed. The given
    word
  Was scarcely from the giver's lips,
Lyle lunges with an angry stroke—
  Is parried—tries again and slips—
His foeman kindly stops and waits;
  Recovered now he comes again;
Swords flash; he strikes an under-stroke,
  But strikes his under-stroke in vain.
The skilled eye of the Fairfax then
  Perceived the demon in the play,
But wished his foe should see that he
  Was ready for him any way.
As storms impetuous break and roar
  Upon some ruggéd, rock-ribbed hill

And fret and fume, because, forsooth,
　They can not have their testy will;
So Lyle now rushed and angry swore
　As stroke met with a fellow stroke,
And circling thousands into cheers—
　As warring clouds peal—sudden broke.
As those spent storms fall into calm
　And settle to their deep repose,
So Lyle now sinks him to the ground
　Beneath the bravest of brave foes.
And mountains unto mountains speak
　As Fairfax' foot rests on his breast.
When sudden calm broods over all,
　His fallen foe he thus addressed:
"Your life is mine.　I grant it now
　On one condition.　That shall be:
Friendship forever shall abide
　Between my fallen foe and me."
Lyle looked and saw upon his face
　A glory from the better land.

"I'm yours henceforth," he said. "I pledge
  The fealty of myself and band."

THE CHRISTMAS FÊTE.

THE Christmas comes to
glad the vale,
New wakened from the
sleep of years,
And pouring forth its latent
wealth
For him whom every heart reveres.
That mind that held the reins of war
And kept the demon in its clasp,
Still reaching forth with newer stroke
And wider sweeps of mental grasp,
Had bid the mountains bring their store
And render homage unto men,

And spread their laps to house and hold
   The teeming hundreds from the glen.
New conquests followed swift his feet;
   With steam he stormed the very height,
And far and wide the landscape laughed
   Beneath his eye's benignant light.
On tree and bush, and grass and rock,
   Close hugging now the prattling creek;
On hill and dale and upland slope
   And boulder, crag and mountain peak,
The snow lies spread all soft and white
   A virgin garb for that sweet day
When all the world with tender love
   Should meet and lift their hearts and
      pray.
The busy song of anvil now
   Is hushed; the panting forge is still;
The ore-banks lie in peace; the beasts
   Range 'round the haystacks on the hill.

The happy children run and laugh
   And stir the old folks with their glee,
Content to have the things that are
   And leave the morrow those to be.
The dusk comes o'er the distant heights
   And spreads its wings across the sky.
The great electric arc-lights gleam
   To guide the foot and glad the eye.
The bell tolls from the steeple's throat
   A chime that sweetens all the air
And bids the thousands meet and greet
   The Christmas fête with praise and
      prayer.
As vast white tents for armies spread,
   All snow-decked now the buildings
      rise,
That are to house and warm the crowds
   That throng beneath the wintry skies.
As mountain rills from pretty glens
   Stream down and gather into one—

Which grows in width and depth and
    strength
  As on it goes to meet the sun;
So from the bright, sweet homes that lie,
  A fringe of glory round the hills,
The multitude now gathers swift—
  Each by the route his good heart wills.
The grand notes of the organ float
  Amid the reaches of the hall,
And touch with rich devotion now
  The tender hearts of one and all.
The pastors who had led their flocks
  Through seasons as they came and
    went,
Now stand in prayer while heads and
  hearts
  In reverent love are near them bent.
The lifted voice is full of thanks
  For blessings through the past year
    sown,

And eager pleadings that the world
   May soon its sovereign Master own,
And rich good will and loving deed
   Adorn each heart and grace each hand
And crown with peace and brotherhood
   The humblest home in every land.
This over, lights flash on the trees
   That rise to meet the children's eyes,
And 'mid their green leaves weave the
     shades
   Of all the rainbow's pretty dyes.
Gift on rich gift hangs tempting there,
   And little hearts are beating fast
With *dreams that are too beautiful,*
   Too golden-bright and sweet to last.
And here and there the couples walk
   With arm in arm—a happy throng!
While oboë and xylophone
   And sweet-voiced violins vie with
     song.

And here there moves a stately form
    And with him one of matchless grace,
Whose bowing heads acknowledge friends
    By scores around with smiling face.
And, as they pass, each reverent heart
    Says to itself a little prayer,
That God may bless with health and joy
    "Glen Mary's" lord and mistress there.
For Fairfax with his charming Jean
    Still loved and kept their trysting place
And with their hands and bounty wreathed
    It daily with a newer grace,
Till far and wide its good fame went
    As stayer of the needy hand—
A royal blessing and a crown
    Of endless glory to the land.
They mingle with the crowding hosts
    And for the nonce are lost to sight;
The surging streams come passing by
    And parting go to left and right.

Now see a man of stalwart mold—
   A giant oak from forests wide—
And with him now a petite form—
   A fairy tripping by his side.
Crede Lyle looks down in eyes all blue
   As waters under laughing skies,
And Cordele owns her heart at rest
   As arm on arm now gently lies.
Two strange lives welded into one,
   By God's grace sweetened and made
     true
To all that's good. The better now
   For what the Past has brought them
     through—
A sturdy tree now settled square
   And ready for a noble growth—
A pretty vine once storm-tossed, now
   In leaf and fruitage putting forth.
A sweet laugh as a child were here
   And glad to see some pretty toy,

Presents us with our cottage maid—
   "Luce" and her noble soldier boy.
They walk and talk and halt to speak
   With some good friend who's passing by,
And tell of how their little home
   Rounds up and out beneath the sky.
And then she sees a little babe
   And runs to kiss it. "Oh! how sweet,
Just see its chubby hands, its eyes,
   And oh! these precious little feet."
The crowds press in, we lose from sight
   Our little Lucy and we hear
The song of children as they march—
   A merry phalanx singing clear.
The hour is on for festal glee—
   And line on line in circles whirls,—
Each father hails his handsome boy,
   Each mother eyes her pretty girls.
The red and blue and white and green
   And orange and the lilac glow;

The pink and black and écru come,
  The gray and mauve and scarlet go.
The streaming ribbons dance and play
  Like leaves before a whirling blast,
And *eyes flash back in winsome way*
  The pretty glances at them cast.
The music fills and thrills the whole,
  And 'mid its lower keys are heard
The bits of laughter break and stir,
  Like notes of some sweet wild-wood
    bird.
The old folks in the neighb'ring booths
  Look out upon the changing scene,
And Reminiscence wakes anew
  The happy days that once have been.
Meanwhile their appetites grow keen
  At savor of the unctious meal,
Whose presence, reeking-sweet and
    glad,
  The lifted curtains now reveal.

The pig, well-roasted, sleek and fat,
　　With apple in his jolly jaws,
And parsley spread—a profuse garb—
　　About him, like a magnet, draws.
Scarce less a monarch of the hour
　　Yon glorious gobbler rears his breast,
And to the hungry, waiting soul
　　Forebodes a longing soon at rest.
The smaller game —'t were useless now
　　To mention—chickens, ducks and geese,
Deer, rabbits, quail, some pheasants, here
　　Opossums lolling in their grease.
The oyster from his native bed
　　Disturbed, a traveller in these parts,
Has come to lend variety
　　And gladden many happy hearts.
The dishes of an endless make
　　Here steam with fruit of every kind
And all the garden and the field
　　Supply to give us peace of mind,

And loaves all fleecy and as sweet
  As ever tempted human thought
Are ranged at intervals, into
  The rarest shapes and sizes wrought.
All things that go to make hearts glad
  And still the craving appetite
Were gathered on the groaning boards
  To crown this glorious Christmas night.
The wine-cup and the whisky-glass—
  Fell wreckers of the human race—
Found here, where Christian hearts were
    met,
  There was for them no fitting place;
But men had manlier ways to glad
  The present than to soak their brains
With fluids that have swept the world
  As great tornadoes sweep the plains.
The agéd now first lead the way,
  Their gray locks crowning honored
    brows,

And reverent bend their heads and say
   The grace a good heart ever vows.
In turn each joins the feasting groups
   Assembled at the tables wide,
And Converse lends her pretty charm
   To usher out the Christmas tide.
Sweet stories of the olden times
   Float from the lips of other days,
And woo the younger folks to vie
   In rich regard and fitting praise;
Or else a maiden's coyness here
   Has tempted some o'er ardent swain,
Secluded and alone, to press
   The suit he's pressed before in vain;
Or pretty mother strokes the hair
   From off her dimpled darling's face,
And glories in its laughing eye,
   Its bounding health and winsome grace.
The feast now done, the hour is come
   To gather 'neath the Christmas trees

And portion to the happy throng
  The gifts as Santa Claus decrees.
The young hearts glow and all their soul
  Expectant sits within their eyes,
Awaiting now to welcome soon
  The rich gifts with glad, little cries.
The busy ushers come and go
  And gladden one by one the whole,
Till all the trees have rendered up
  Their fruit to ladder and to pole.
Then sounds the proclamation far
  For peace and order once again.
The surging crowds obey and rest
  As billows calmed upon the main.
From where the dais sinks from sight
  Behind the curtains in the rear,
The stately form and loving face
  Of My Lord Fairfax now appear.
He waves his hand, the crowds, now still,
  All bend to catch his every word.

His voice, sweet toned and clear ran out
   So that each list'ning burgher heard:
"Friends," so he speaks, "within your
      thought
There lies the memory of a vow,
That once you made on upland crag
   And lowland lea; where is it now?
Here by my side your leader stands,
   A brother to my heart and soul
And partner full; o'er you he wields
   With me an even half-control.
Led on by wooings of that love
   That streams from God to sweeten
      life
And still all cause for hate and gloom
   Or further internecine strife,
We come to-night to bless ourselves
   In blessing you. For we believe
That surplus wealth is but a trust
   Bestowed of God that we may give

His bounty back to those whose sweat
  Has won it from the grasp of earth,
And pass to God with hands as clean
  As when we came from Him at birth.
Who lives alone for hoarded pelf
  Is but a hunger-smitten beast,
Whose gnawing vitals famish 'mid
  The glowing plenty of the feast.
He misses all the subtle, sweet
  And radiant joy of those who live
And follow Him who taught, 'It is
  More blest to give than to receive.'
So all these acres spreading wide,
  These mines that teem with hidden
    worth,
These forges threat'ning to the skies,
  These buildings hugging close the
    earth,
Henceforth, in part are yours as ours;
  His share awaits each freeman here;

For him who saves, henceforth, my friends,
  The way to plenty now is clear.
Our aim is for our mutual good,
  Yourselves and us alike to lift.
(My noble wife unites her voice)
  Receive, my friends, your Christmas
      gift."
The welkin rang and glad hearts wept,
  The preacher rose and raised the song,
"Praise God from whom all blessings
      flow,"
  And with a prayer dismissed the
      throng.